Throw the Bouquet

An April May Snow Psychic Adventure

By

M. Scott Swanson

"A true friend never gets in your way unless you happen to be going down."

-Arnold Glasow

Dedicated to

Paulette A. Swanson

April May Snow Titles

Throw the Bouquet   (Prequel #1)

Throw the Cap   (Prequel #2)

Throw the Dice   (Prequel #3)

Throw the Elbow   (Prequel #4)

Throw the Fastball   (Prequel #5)

Throw the Gauntlet   (Prequel #6)

Throw the Hissy   (Prequel #7)

Foolish Aspirations   (Novel #1)

Foolish Beliefs   (Novel #2)

Chapter 1

I check the time on my phone again. The evening has slowed to a crawl, and the backbeat of the country cover band jackhammers my fraying nerves.

Sighing, I evaluate the condition of my girls. They're loud, hungry for attention and peer affirmation, and in varying degrees of undress. They need to be in bed. I don't relish the prospect of marshaling the unruly lot back to the hotel. The very thought of the whining and complaints sure to ensue when I announce playtime is over threatens to bring on one of my debilitating migraines.

Moments like this remind me why I'm ready to leave this chapter of my life in the rearview mirror. My friends try to convince me I'll miss it. They remind me I'm the best woman for any job.

That's the truth. I'm the absolute best. You can ask anyone who knows me. Mama says it's not bragging if it's a fact.

But will I miss it? Like a toothache.

I lift my lemonade on the rocks to my lips, I hood my eyelids to demonstrate I'm as wasted as the rest of my crew. They like their margaritas frozen, while I prefer mine on the rocks, so I don't get a brain freeze. At least, that's what they've all heard me say at least a hundred times. The lemonade is a little trick I learned by the second bachelorette party I hosted.

Trying to keep track of everyone is a complete pain when you're sober, but darn near impossible buzzed. I don't always like all the women in our group tonight, but I'd feel bad if one of them gets hurt or lost.

Probably.

The bride, Susan Esposito, soon to be Taylor if she doesn't break her neck first, is trying to climb her high-backed stool to dance on the table for the second time. "Lisa! Don't let her get up there again." I shout over the loud country music.

Lisa erupts into laughter as she grabs Susan's waistband with one hand. The daiquiri, in her other hand, sloshes down the front of her already stained yellow dress. "But she wants to dance!"

"She can dance at the reception after she's married."

Lisa pushes her lower lip out, forming a pout. I think she believes it makes her look cute and endearing. I want to slap the pout off her face.

I hop off my stool, slide by Lisa, and take Susan's hand. "Come on. We can't have your daddy pushing you down the aisle in a wheelchair because you broke your leg."

Susan slaps at my hand. "Stop it, April. You're not the only one who can tabletop dance. When did you become such a killjoy?"

Susan is right. Some of my exploits during my undergraduate degree at the University of Alabama would make the devil blush. I'm not proud of it. Well, maybe a little, as some were epic, but the killjoy comment is just harsh.

I'm not a wet blanket. I'm just in the process of maturing. That's what paying for—taking out enormous loans would be more accurate—for three years of law school will do to you. Age you. Plus, the whole go to the bar at ten PM, spend all your money on overpriced alcohol, scream last week's tired story at your friend over the music, puke in the alley, giggle for no good reason all the way home, and wake up feeling like a truck ran over you—I'm not sure why, but I've sort of lost interest in it.

I wouldn't be at this party except half the women were in my sorority the year I was the chapter president. Susan, the bride, was my personal pledge in my senior year. You understand I couldn't beg her off when she asked me to be her bridesmaid.

Standing as a bridesmaid is always an honor. To me, an even greater compliment of trust is being asked to host the bachelorette party. I've been a bridesmaid in twenty-three weddings and the hostess of sixteen bachelorette parties. I think the shine of distinction for both has worn off for me.

You heard me right. This is the sixteenth tour of duty as the captain of the good girl's faux night of debauchery. Don't get me wrong, there's a few in the crew who lean hard to the dark side that I need to keep a constant eye on.

Melissa Owens, for example, is one who leans toward the naughty girls' club. She's been married for three years and has a toddler at home. But her hungry stare is so intense it might as well be tracing a red dot on every passing cowboy's jeans right where his zipper bottoms out. I wouldn't trust her for a minute away from the rest of the group. Nothing messes up a tasteful wedding like someone sleeping with someone they shouldn't have and their man getting all loud about it during the reception.

We are in Nashville. That explains all the men walking around in jeans a little on the tight side. That's part of the reason I've hosted so many times. Nashville, not the tight jeans.

Five years ago, when Patricia Lloyd, my big sister in the sorority, asked me to host her bachelorette party, I was clueless. Luckily, I have a second cousin in Nashville who helped me put together a day-long itinerary. To this day, that first-party receives awed whispers of praise within the halls of my sorority.

Since then, when any of my sisters are engaged to be married, it's always, "Oh, April must do your bachelorette party." It's hard to say no when you're famous for something. I'm sure some nights Jimmy Buffett doesn't feel like singing Margaritaville, but it's his thing. Right?

Besides, I like Nashville. It fits me. Most of the girls don't know that about me. We're not that kind of close.

I sit back on my stool and watch them in their shiny, just purchased cowgirl boots and too short denim skirts. Suburban girls of privilege who have only interacted with other suburban girls of privilege their entire lives. They are just playing country girl tonight—awkwardly. Me? I'm a country girl trying to sever ties with my roots.

I'm at odds with my upbringing. I believe in global warming, so I drive a hybrid. But antique muscle cars give me goosebumps.

I also love the commanding view a jacked-up pick-up truck provides.

I certainly believe in feminist causes. But I still love it when a man lays an aggressive, hungry kiss on me. The type of kiss that shows he'll die if he can't have me right then. I'm always like, "You do what you think you need to, Mister. I'll put you in your place if your hands land somewhere I don't want them."

Because of these things, my daddy says I'm a dichotomy. I think it just makes me interesting.

A calloused hand glides across the back of my shoulder. Swiveling on my barstool, I come face to face with a not unattractive fellow twenty-something who looks like he has a secret he wants to share.

"Hey, beautiful. Do you want some company?" My new friend asks.

Yes, it's a pick-up line. I'm not what you would call a 'Classic Beauty.' But I can catch a man's eye on most any occasion I wish. Nana Hirsch tells me I got the 'It' factor from my Grandpa. It always makes me feel a bit awkward when she makes the comment, and I'm not positive what 'It' is. Still, guys like the weekend cowboy presently favoring me with 'Sexy Eyes' stick to me like ants to spilled honey.

"Yeah, my dance card is sort of full tonight, cowboy." I point to the fifteen women in my care.

"They can't do the kind of dancing I want to do with you." He moves in close enough for me to smell the liquid courage on his breath. Whiskey and cola, I'm quite sure.

"No. All my girlfriends know the electric slide." I give him my slightly confused, innocent face. Sorry. I can be sort of a tease even when it's not going anywhere.

"Not the way I do the electric slide, baby."

Cute. A cowboy wannabe with a double entendre. Under different circumstances, but tonight is not about me.

"Listen. Be nice and move along. I'm busy here."

His brow lowers with a frown, and his ears turn radish red. Then his smile reappears as he inspects the rest of the women at our table. "Do you mind if I go talk to her?" He points at Melissa Owens.

"Dude, can you not take a hint?" I twirl my finger. "Girl's party. Female bonding. No boys allowed. Get it? Nobody at this table is going home with you tonight."

He glares at me, and I feel the energy in the air change. "You can't tell me who I can and can't talk to."

I pull my handbag into my lap. "The best thing about being a woman is my handbag. I can hide things in my handbag that you can't hide in your tight jeans."

Cowboy wannabe considers my comment. Given his confused expression, I expect to see smoke smoldering out his ears at any moment.

I hop down from my high-backed stool and begin to unzip my purse. "Would you like to say hello to my little friend?"

He grins as his eyes scan hungrily over the women in my party. "Which one?"

Man, I'd been waiting to use that line for over five years, and I wasted it on this numbskull. How can this cowboy wannabe not know that line?

On second thought, he doesn't seem to be the sharpest tool in the shed.

I rest my hand lightly on his chest and then pull a pen from my purse. "Listen. Not tonight." I scribble a phone number on a cocktail napkin. "But give me a call in the morning. Maybe we can get together and hang. Cool?"

He studies the consolation prize before tucking the napkin into his shirt pocket. "Okay. That'll work. I'll talk to you tomorrow."

I wave my fingers as he walks off. Hopefully, the number I made up isn't in use. I'd hate to be the person unlucky enough to be stuck explaining to the psycho cowboy he's been duped.

There's a collective groan from my party as the lights come up, signaling the end of our night's frivolity. Talk about catching a break. Now I won't have to play the bad guy.

"All right, buddy system. Let's head out for the bus." I grab hold of Susan's hand and make a point to buddy up with her from the start. Another lesson learned. All the girls are valued, but the show can't go on without the bride. Everyone else is replaceable.

I confirm all the girls are in their rooms before retiring to mine. The plan is to catch five hours of shut-eye, get into our sweatpants, eat breakfast, and head down to Birmingham in the morning for the wedding rehearsal and dinner.

I play it safe all the way and bunk with Susan. Unfortunately, after I get her makeup off and lead her to bed, she begins to sober up.

"What have I done?" Her lips part as she stares at the wall.

I glance at her as I fluff my pillow, "Trust me, you didn't do anything to be ashamed of tonight. Besides, even if you did, I'd have broken any phones in the bar."

Her eyes lock on to me as if she just now realizes I'm in the room, "No. I mean, what have I done by getting engaged."

This is the first time I even have a hint Susan isn't entirely thrilled about being the future Ms. Jackson Taylor. Not to mention, I'm not the best person to have the conversation with because I only know her fiancé, Jackson, in passing.

"Aren't you excited to be marrying Jackson?" I ask tentatively.

"Maybe. Oh, I don't know. Do you think God will punish us if we end up getting a divorce? I mean, after giving our vows."

I can't speak for God, but I'm sure Susan's daddy will be tore up after the small fortune he must be spending on the opulent wedding. "Isn't it more important to decide if marrying Jackson makes you happy?"

"Forever is a long time, April." Susan locks eyes with me. "A long time."

Yes, it is. Three years of law school seemed like forever. Saying you're going to live with one person for the rest of your life, just being honest, that's a big one to wrap my head around. "I don't want to influence you one way or the other, but don't forget, until you actually say I do, you can still say I don't."

Tears begin to run down Susan's face. "I'm just so scared."

I've seen this reaction from several brides in the preceding five years. For the life of me, I can't empathize. When it's my time to marry, if I'm not insanely ecstatic, I'll call the whole thing off. Especially if I want to cry about it. "Why?"

Her hands drop to the mattress. "It's just the unknown. Who knows how this is going to end?"

"Y'all dated for a couple of years. There can't be that much unknown left."

"But you never know how this is going to end up. Whether we stay happily married for seventy years or get an annulment after seventy days."

Fair. I've learned the only certainty in relationships is uncertainty. "It's one day at a time, Susan. One day at a time."

I sit up reluctantly, swing my sore feet from my bed, walk over to her, lay her back down on her pillow, and tuck her in. "I'm sure you two will be thrilled over your new life together. Try to get some sleep."

When I turn out the light, I lay in bed awake, thinking. Will they be happy? Has Susan made a wise decision in selecting Jackson as her life partner? I just don't know. I hope so. I want her to be happy. But I'm unable to assuage the churning feeling in my gut and electrical pinpricks that dance across my skin.

Regardless of how Susan will decide, I promise myself something in the dark. April May Snow will never cry the night before her wedding day. If I can't smile, laugh, and act a fool at my wedding —if I ever decide to get married—my fiancé will see my tail feathers shake as I walk out the door signaling 'deuces' over my shoulder. Life's too short to be with the wrong guy.

Chapter 2

I'm ready to offload the girls to the high-dollar wedding planners when we reach Birmingham. Since they appointed me defacto room mom, I was treated to everyone's complaints about hangovers, lost items, and unconsented social media posts on the five-hour bus ride to Birmingham. As a special reward, I had the honor of holding Mary Jo Newton's hair when we pulled over on the shoulder of interstate sixty-five south of Franklin so she could puke her breakfast out. The nationwide glow of the Southern Belle charm is a little dimmer after that moment of discomfiture.

The bus driver unloads our luggage, and I hand him a hundred-dollar bill. I know it doesn't begin to make up for suffering our group this morning. Still, at least I'm acknowledging it's an unenviable assignment.

"You got a pack full of trouble there," the bus driver comments with a smile as he points to the disorganized mass of women congregating at the front desk.

"They just don't get out much." I favor him my sweetest, 'That will be all now' smile.

"They don't know how fortunate they are to have an older sister to take care of them." He tips his cap. "Good luck with that."

I stare a hole in the driver's back as he steps onto the bus. Older sister? I'm the same age as most of these girls. I'm not anyone's older sister.

"April!"

Susan stomps toward me. She fixes her face for a throwdown.

"They said we don't have a reservation." Her brown eyes open wide. "Did the bus driver drop us off at the wrong hotel or what?"

"We're at the right hotel." I slide past her without any further explanation on my way to the front desk.

The pretty young desk clerk appears flustered as the girls pepper her with questions about why they don't have reservations and what they're supposed to do without rooms. The clerk's head jerks from side to side—her mouth opens and closes. She's unable to get a word in before the next woman lobs an aggressive question at her.

"Ma'am." My level tone draws her attention. Her shoulders relax as her eyes plead for me to bring much-needed sanity to the situation. "Please check under Esposito-Taylor."

"Esposito-Taylor? You're hyphenating your name?" Melissa cackles.

"No, I'm not!" Susan yells back.

I want to ignore them, but I'm afraid we're one ill-advised adjective away from a catfight. Hotels that are four-hundred-dollars a night at double occupancy don't take kindly to catfights in their lobby.

I hiss over my shoulder. "Cool it. It's just the name for the reservations." I wave my finger at the group of women. "The room block is for both the bride and the groom's families."

"Here it is!"

I try to erase the irritation from my facial expression as I turn back to the clerk.

"There's supposed to be a block of fifty rooms. We'll need eight of the rooms now if we can check in early."

Susan Esposito, the bride, is an adorable girl. When she first pledged our sorority, she was painfully bookish and shy to the point of awkwardness. Truth be known, if Susan hadn't been a third-generation legacy, she never would've received an offer. Susan is smart, without the ability to effectively hide it like I can, and she can be judgmental about the naughtier things that go on in Greek society. Two things sorority sisters don't like—people who are smarter than them and people who judge them.

It's one of the reasons why I took her on as a little sister. I knew the other girls would've tormented her relentlessly.

Don't get me wrong, I'm not one of those people who always root for the underdog or feel the need to protect the weak and vulnerable. I just like her honesty. We are similar in that manner. Although our delivery is entirely different. Susan's honesty runs on the sweet and diplomatic side while mine is sarcastic and blunt.

I lean over the counter and point at the room diagram the clerk is trying to decipher. Running my finger down one of the hallways marked reserved, I point out which rooms I want for the bride's party and where I wish Susan and my room to be located.

"Thank you," the clerk gushes, "I wasn't sure where to start. Would you like two keys?"

"That would be perfect. Thank you." I favor the clerk with a smile. Her anxiety is replaced with calm confidence, her proficiency evident, once my flock of overindulged princesses is no longer verbally assaulting her.

I dole out room card packets to the seven pairs of roommates. "You've got exactly four hours until the dress rehearsal. They have a nice pool out back if any of you brought your swimsuits, and there's a gym on the first floor." I point at the carpeted floor. "But I expected everybody here and dressed at five-o'clock sharp for the bus. Understand?"

There are enough head nods and mumbled yeses to make me believe they understand I'm not in the mood to brook any deviations from the schedule.

"You want to go catch a shower?" I ask Susan.

"I thought you'd never ask."

Chapter 3

The thread connecting all the women I know personally in Susan's party is our sorority from the University of Alabama in Tuscaloosa. It's not unusual for one of our sisters to marry in Birmingham. As the most populous city in Alabama, a fair number of their families live in Birmingham.

But we were all surprised Jackson and Susan's wedding would be in Birmingham. Jackson is a Tuscaloosa local, and Susan's family owns a massive precast concrete wall operation just outside of Tuscaloosa. For those reasons, I thought their wedding venue would be close to the university.

What I forgot is Susan's daddy never misses an opportunity to promote the family business. A business he developed from the humble beginnings of a single concrete mixer-truck to a regional precast powerhouse. He isn't Harbert sort of wealthy, but he sure isn't hurting, and Susan never wants for anything.

If the apple doesn't fall far from the tree, the Esposito family tree must be rooted on a steep slope. Susan rolled a good distance once she fell from the family tree. Where her daddy is all about the money and the appearance of wealth, Susan isn't wired that way. I admire her for that.

I holler into the bathroom as she takes her shower. "What time is your momma supposed to be here?"

"She said no later than three."

"And you're sure she's got the dress?"

She laughs. "April. Come on now."

"I'm just saying she can be a little flighty."

"I made her text me a picture of it in her car before she left."

See? Smart girl. "Okay. I'm going to go get a bottle of water. You want anything?"

"A ginger ale, please."

Yuck. Susan's stomach must be bothering her. I decide to see if I can dig up some Ritz crackers or Saltines at the snack bar, too. "Okay, I'll be back soon."

Taking a break to get snacks allows me to call Alecia Harbuck. Alecia, a.k.a., the schedule dominatrix. Alecia is, in the circle of recent and soon to be brides, considered the best wedding planner in Alabama north of Montgomery. She's creative, organized, and determined. She insists each of her brides' wedding days be the most luxurious show of the season—even if it means sucking every ounce of joy out of the proceedings.

Alecia is the main reason I volunteered to coordinate the bachelorette party. Initially, Alecia wanted control of the bachelorette party schedule. I assured her I had it handled, and I promised to have the girls in Birmingham no later than noon for the rehearsal dinner.

Why would anyone volunteer to oversee planning a bachelorette party when the bride's parents are prepared to pay a wedding coordinator? That's a fair question. Let's just say that enduring six hours of drunk women in cowgirl boots screaming "Hey Y'all" out of a party bus while 'Save a Horse Ride a Cowboy' and 'Independence Day' play on an endless loop is what bachelorette parties are supposed to be. In contrast, the luncheonette Alecia planned for Tammy Mercury's wedding last year? Saying it was a snooze fest is exceptionally generous.

"You're late." Alecia's tone can cut diamonds.

"We had to keep stopping for one of the girls who wasn't feeling well. I've got Susan taking a shower now." I tell her as I peruse the well-stocked hotel snack collection.

"I need both of you at the church within the hour. Cynthia will come over to collect the rest of the bride's party at five."

I pick up a short sleeve of Ritz crackers. "We'll be there on time."

"Her mother still hasn't shown up with the dress."

I grin, thinking about the picture Susan made her mother send. "We're good there. You worry too much."

"I get paid to worry, so the bride doesn't have to."

I can't argue with that. "Uh-huh."

"Thank you again for getting them all back down from that stupid party. It always makes me nervous when they have a function outside of the wedding city."

I can visualize Alecia's hawkish features. Her blonde mane pulled back severely, and a judgmental frown stretched across her lips. The same face that sucked any remnants of joy out of Tammy Mercury's so-called bachelorette luncheon. "No worries. I'll see you within the hour."

I open the door to our room. Susan is sitting on her bed with a towel wrapped around her, a second turbaned loosely on her head.

The door slams behind me, and I grin at her. "Alecia sends her love."

"Did she say if Jackson was at the church yet?"

Darn. I was so relieved I completed the most challenging part of my job—herding cats—that I hadn't bothered to ask about the groom. "She didn't mention it."

"Oh."

I hand her the ginger ale and crackers while I study her face. Something isn't right. Unfortunately, I'm not sure of the best way to ask what has her troubled. Susan has become such a bundle of nerves, asking a question seems like poking at wires on an explosive device. I'm just not sure it's something I want to do. Besides, her momma is on the way. Mommas love asking their daughters uncomfortable questions. Right?

That's one of the things I hate about being a friend. There's always a fine line between caring and overbearing. You must be careful not to step over the boundary. To make it worse, the boundary continually changes with the status of your relationship.

Family is totally different. A family crosses well-established boundaries any time they darn well please and don't worry about the ramifications in the least. Friends aren't family. Even when friends claim you've become family, you're not.

I open my water and take a few sips as I continue to watch Susan warily. *Just hop in the shower, April. Just jump in the shower. You've got to get ready.*

My stupid curiosity gets the best of me again. I reach for Susan's ginger ale and unscrew the cap for her. "You're not yourself. What's bothering you?"

She raises her gaze to mine, and her eyes betray her desperation. She rocks slowly as tears threaten to fall. "I just don't know. I should be all happy and laughing, but I have this bubbling in my stomach. Something is just off."

Uh oh. "Off with you? Or off like with the wedding?"

A tear streams down her cheek. "I don't know, that's just it."

I'm trying to play it cool, but my apprehensions about Susan's mood last night are causing me alarm. "I don't mean to badger you, Susan. We need to figure this out and soon. If this is just wedding jitters, fine. But if Jackson said something to you or—"

"Jackson didn't say anything! Why is everyone always thinking the worst of him?"

I raise my hands, palm out. "I just think whatever the issue is, we should get it resolved before the wedding."

She draws a long, ragged breath, "Yeah. We will." She gestures toward the bathroom. "You better get a shower. We don't want to get on the bad side of Alecia."

"I'm not afraid of Alecia."

Susan snorts a tear-choked laugh. "You're not, but I am."

Chapter 4

The downtown parish in Birmingham is beautiful. One thing about the Catholics, when they decide to build a church, by golly, they construct a cathedral. I've been to two other weddings at this church, but the vaulted ceilings and stained-glass windows never cease to impress me.

"There you are." Alecia stomps toward us, her five-foot-ten frame balanced perfectly on four-inch stiletto heels. "I was wondering if you were going to make a fashionably late appearance."

Alecia gathers Susan's hands in hers and holds them at waist height while she inspects her. "So, that's a cute dress."

It isn't a compliment. It's easy to read Alecia doesn't believe the mid-thigh cotton print dress is appropriate for the rehearsal and dinner. I think Susan looks adorable in it. The dress fits her personality to a 'T'.

"Is Jackson here?" Susan peers over Alecia's shoulder.

Alecia's eyes narrow, causing her features to appear even more severe. "He's around here somewhere. Your parents haven't made it yet."

"We told her parents to be here by five. You said you wanted to talk to the bride and groom at four." I remind her.

Alecia glares at me. "Yes, well, I had an expectation that they might arrive earlier."

Everyone seems to be a little overly tense today, even for a wedding. "I'm just gonna go grab a seat in the back pew."

In case you haven't figured it out yet, I don't do well with passive-aggressive personalities. Don't get me wrong, I have all the respect in the world for Alecia. I've seen her work enough to know her designs reflect an inspired artist. Her planning is ruthlessly methodical, and she is on a constant quest for perfection. If you've hired Alecia, you can be confident she will do everything possible to ensure your wedding is the topic of everyone's discussion that month. Alecia can also make sure your wedding guests never use the phrase 'A good time' when describing your event to their friends.

I sit on the last row of pews. I can barely hear Susan and Alecia's voices. It's a little warm in the chapel, and I struggle to keep my eyes open. I'm either going for a walk or curling up on the red pew cushion and taking a nap.

I decide not to embarrass myself. I go for a walk in the much cooler hallway in search of a water fountain.

Old churches are built for praying, not creature comforts. Bathrooms and water coolers can be as sparse and as welcome as an oasis in the desert.

As I take a few sips of stale water the fountain offers, I decide to check my makeup in the small bathroom next to the fountain. I tossed my makeup on exceptionally quick at the hotel so we wouldn't be late.

The bathroom is a cramped one-seater. The air hangs heavy and thick as if there are no air vents. As feared, my makeup looks like some of my middle school attempts.

Whatever is eating at Susan must be catching. I'm not sure if it's just sympathetic nerves or what, but my skin tingles so intensely I begin to scratch at my arms. The only time my skin crawls like this is when...

No. It wouldn't be that.

I reapply my eyeliner. Susan seemed perfectly fine last night until the moment we were alone when she became anxious but offered no explanation.

Digging for my lipstick, something she said comes back to me. "Everybody thinks the worst of Jackson." Who is everybody, and why do they think the worst of him? Is Susan apprehensive about getting married or her marital choice? The skin on my shoulders and arms feels like spiders are racing over it as I fix my lipstick.

There is a vast difference between being nervous about getting married and worrying you are hitching your future to the wrong man. Huge!

A loud, hostile sounding masculine voice interrupts my musings, and I jerk to attention, dropping my lipstick. As I pull the lipstick out of the sink, I can clearly hear one side of what I take to be a phone conversation.

"No, it will all be taken care of. Stop worrying."

I lean closer to the bathroom door. I clench the lipstick tight in my right hand.

"You know I'm good for it. Have I let you down in the past?" There is a brief pause. "They know that wasn't my fault."

Who was that voice? It's vaguely familiar.

"Listen, you'll just have to trust me. But don't call me on this number again. It's too easy to trace, and I don't want to have to explain your calls to anyone."

It's none of your business, April. Finish touching up your makeup and let it go.

"Right. I don't know, a week and then probably another thirty days." Another short span of silence. "Come on, five weeks, and you'll have everything. If you do that, you won't get a dime."

Stupid curiosity. I'm going to have to step out and identify whose voice I'm listening to. Placing my hand on the doorknob, I begin to turn it.

"Yes, I can call you after it's done."

Something about the phrase "after it's done" chills my blood. I release the doorknob. My curiosity chickens out. Thank goodness.

I sit on the toilet seat to replay the conversation in my head. It seems less threatening and relatively harmless the second time. I'm just anxious, like Susan, and my mind is formulating silly conspiracy theories.

I finally step out of the bathroom, and an unexpected motion in my right peripheral squeezes the breath out of me. I whirl toward the water fountain where a medium height man with sandy hair angles his head as he watches me with apparent amusement.

"I didn't mean to spook you. I was just getting a drink of this nasty water."

A chill runs up my spine. The man's voice is unmistakably the same as the phone caller I eavesdropped on. It takes a moment for his face to move from familiar to identified. "It's definitely not holy water, Jackson."

Jackson's smile spreads slowly. It makes the hairs on the back of my neck stand up. "If it were holy water, I'd be writhing in pain for sure."

Is that a confession or a joke? Taking in the dangerous smile on his face, I can believe either. "I thought Alecia was giving you and Susan the last-minute instructions."

He gestures back toward the chapel. "I'm sort of procrastinating. That chick is such a ball-buster I decided to wait until the rest of my crew gets here."

I certainly understand where he's coming from, but if the wedding coordinator needs to bust balls and you're the groom, ducking your responsibilities isn't optional. "The sooner we get in there, the sooner the coordinator will be done."

"I'll keep my balls safe and wait for back up if it's all the same to you." He gives me a dismissive pat on the shoulder.

Visions run like wildfire through my mind as my clairvoyance apparently skips into telepathy. That's a first.

Vertigo strikes me stronger than ever before. My stomach turns and lurches as if I've chased a rotten turkey burger with a jalapeno juice shot. Swaying, I barely catch myself before I collapse, and stumble to the left.

Jackson grabs my wrist and supports me. Another kaleidoscope of colors, smells, and sounds flash through my brain.

"Steady now. Did you girls not eat this morning after your night out?"

Fudge biscuit! I struggle to straighten myself as Jackson releases my wrist. "Yes. Just not enough sleep."

He studies my face. I'm struck with the frightening and irrational idea that Jackson somehow is aware I just read the horrible thoughts bouncing around in his head.

Time slows as we stare at one another. I can hear my heartbeat in my ears, and I hope my nervous swallowing is not as loud as it seems.

No. Jackson doesn't know. Given the brutality and perversion of the visions, I'd expect him to act immediately to silence me if he believed I were aware of his twisted sexual thoughts.

"On second thought, I might as well get this over with." Jackson twitches his eyebrows upward as if to say, 'How about it?'

We walk in silence back to the chapel. Thankfully, the nasty burning sensation in my stomach subsides. Still, my mind retains the images which flashed across my mind too quickly to decipher fully. The ugly, brutal visions repeat on a loop in my mind. My knees turn to jelly as each deviant image clarifies itself.

Jackson's thoughts were some sexual version of role-playing is what I try to convince myself. I know some of my girlfriends joke about role-playing as a way of spicing up their sex life.

I don't really get it, though. I suppose I'm sort of a prude in that arena. My idea of role-playing is for a hot shirtless guy to wash my car and offer to fill it up for free—the gas tank.

The woman bound, nude in a weird position with some sort of a ball looking thing in her mouth, didn't look comfortable. I couldn't imagine that ever getting my motor running, but hey to each their own if they have one of those safe words or whatever.

The part of Jackson's thoughts that really freaks me out is the girl in his vision is me. I'm not sure if that's something my mind did or if it was Jackson's. Either way, it's incredibly disturbing to me and makes me feel like I have a thick layer of slime on my skin. I feel violated, and I was the one who read his mind without his permission.

"There you are," Alecia scolds as she approaches us. Her facial expression changes from aggravation to questioning as she nears. "Is everything okay?"

"Yeah. April and I ran into each other at the water fountain."

"Everything's good. I'm just looking forward to dinner."

"Okay." Alecia's doubting expression makes me feel dirty even though I haven't done anything wrong. "How about you two stay in the chapel until the rehearsal is over?"

I reclaim my seat in one of the back pews. I'm profoundly troubled on two counts.

First, and selfishly the most important to me is the fact my carefully concealed clairvoyance has skipped the rails into telepathy. My 'Gifts' are a curse I've dealt with since the age of eight, and I work ridiculously hard to keep my mind partitioned to limit it so I can lead a normal life.

The last thing I need in my life is one more bit of weirdness to have to hide from the rest of the world. What I wouldn't give to be normal like all my friends.

Second, it's going to take a lot of time and energy to unpack the visions I unintentionally gleaned from Jackson. Hopefully, they'll seem less repulsive now that I'm prepared for the perverse topics. I'm sure it just caught me off guard.

If it were possible, I'd go back in time and avoid touching Jackson. Some things are best left unknown.

Get over yourself April.

The visions that flashed between our minds were merely a collection of random thoughts. I couldn't truly glean anything of actual value, except the man's taste run heavy on the carnal and extreme side. Last I checked that isn't necessarily a crime to think those things—acting out on those thoughts would be a matter decided in a court of law.

It's my own fault. I concentrated on Jackson because of Susan's statement and her general anxiety. Concern for Susan put my focus on her fiancé, and when the opportunity arose, my mind wired to his briefly. That must be it.

Over the years, I've become very proficient at blocking my clairvoyance. But if I focus on an individual for an extended period, a conduit connects between me and the individual, and something as simple as feeling an item they've had contact with cranks on the faucet. This was the first time the article I touched was the actual person.

I feel dirty, not just from what I found in Jackson's mind, but because I peered in without his knowledge. Jackson's brain is his own sovereign sacrosanct. It was wrong for me to eavesdrop on him. Unfortunately, it's just as hard for me to forget someone else's thoughts as it is to ignore something I've seen or heard first-hand.

One thing for sure, Jackson is no choir boy. If family and friends are telling Susan he isn't marriage material, it's because they know about his lifestyle. The question is, does Susan know, and if she does, is she blinded by her love? Blind love will break your heart every time.

Reluctantly I run the disturbing visions through my head once again. I'm right. They're equally repulsive the third and fourth viewing, but they don't have the dramatic, visceral effect on me as they did the first time.

To say I'm conflicted is an understatement. How I came to the knowledge of Jackson's darkest thoughts is wrong. Yet, now that I know them, it seems equally unforgivable not to share the ill-gotten information with Susan.

Mr. and Mrs. Esposito arrive with their eldest daughter Courtney. Courtney decided not to attend the bachelorette party because of the little bundle attached to her back. Her daughter Maisie is still breastfeeding, and Courtney isn't comfortable leaving her with pumped breast milk.

Susan made it known to me; she felt Courtney was overly cautious. It hurt her deeply that "her own sister" didn't attend her bachelorette party. I figure, since neither of us is a mother yet, we should reserve judgment. But Susan can't let it go that easily.

Family stuff. What are you going to say?

It makes me appreciate only having brothers. I'm not sure I'd want to share the princess crown with a sister.

Mr. and Mrs. Esposito immediately go to Jackson, Susan, and Alecia. I leave the pew, walk up to Courtney, and give her a hug.

"I see you got my sister here in one piece as you promised," Courtney says.

"I'm usually able to keep my promises."

Courtney exhales as if she's exhausted. "I just hope in a few days we're not all wishing the bus had broken down on the way back from Nashville."

I'd say Courtney isn't giving the union a vote of confidence. "That bad?"

"Who knows? I'm sure it's just me and all these post-pregnancy hormones bouncing around. Plus, with Lucas being on another deployment, my nerves are shot."

Courtney's husband, Lucas Jones, is a captain in the Marines. If he's on another deployment, that'll make his third since they've been married. "I'm sure it's a big sister's prerogative to be skeptical if any man is good enough for her baby sister."

Courtney lets out a short laugh and covers her mouth. "Oh, I have a mild case of the doubts." She gestures toward her parents. "They look all cozy up there talking as a group, but Momma doesn't have a kind word to say about Jackson, and I think Daddy would rather shoot him than talk to him."

"Why do they feel that way about him?"

Courtney scans around us quickly, I suspect to make sure no one is in earshot. She continues in a whisper, "I'll tell you, but I'll warn you not to mention it to Susan if you don't want her going ballistic on you."

"Well, thanks for the warning, but if it's important, she'll probably hear it from me too regardless of the temper tantrum."

Courtney considers my comment and smiles, "You're a good friend, April. I'm glad you're in her life," She leans closer to me. "Nobody knows what Jackson does for a living. He says he's some sort of financial advisor, but we can't confirm that. What we can confirm is that he doesn't have a regular nine-to-five job. It's all too weird. Sometimes he tells Susan they're broke and the next thing you know he'll drive up in a new sports car. It's shady."

"Maybe his income fluctuates. Most of my family are entrepreneurs, so I understand how his income could vary wildly from month to month."

"Daddy certainly thinks he's an entrepreneur, but a gambler and Momma has started to say he must be a drug dealer. If I were to pitch in my two cents, I'd guess a male escort wannabe."

My mouth falls open, "Courtney. Seriously?"

She shakes her head, vehemently. "I don't know April. But something doesn't add up." She glares toward Jackson. "I swear if he does anything to my sister, I'll beat him to death with a rubber mallet."

I almost snicker but repress it at the last second. Courtney usually has this angelic ultra-positive quality about her. To hear her threaten violence, and especially a violent act she's thought through while rocking her baby in her arms both shocks and amuses me.

Maisie stirs. Courtney pulls the baby blanket further from her daughter's face. "Are you hungry, Maisie?"

Maisie's bottom lip trembles as her forehead wrinkles. She's the prettiest baby I've ever seen.

In wonderment, I watch Courtney and Maisie. The love between the two is evident and fills me with emotion. Courtney is in her element. She's a woman who knows exactly what she wants from life.

"Life is a series of trade-offs and sacrifices, so make sure your decisions are deliberate." Grandpa Snow coached that to my twin brothers and me every summer when we were on the farm. It was good solid advice. But not the easiest to follow.

I sacrificed a lot to earn a law degree. A tremendous amount of time and effort, for one. Financial freedom because of the loans, for another. To obtain the level of success I want, I'll end up delaying marriage until I'm older. I'm good with these trade-offs. But I'd be lying if I said there isn't a little yearning tug when I see a pretty baby. I don't want to be a homemaker, and Lord knows I'm not ready to raise a child, but some days I have a pang for the sacrifices still to be laid on the altar of success.

"You want to hold her?"

Yes. No. "I'm not very good with kids."

Courtney favors me with a sweet smile. "I think you would be wonderful with kids. I'm positive you'll end up being that mom where all the other kids tell your daughters how lucky they are to have such a cool mom."

I can't help but smile. I know Courtney is just being nice because that's what Courtney does. But it still gives me a warm feeling in my heart.

During the rehearsal, I watch Jackson closely, alert for any hints of what has made Susan's family doubt his character.

True, he's arrogant and standoffish, but that isn't unusual for a young man under thirty born into wealth. Especially not a young man who has some decent looks about him.

I don't witness any overt ugliness toward Susan or her family. He doesn't like Alecia, but many men don't care for women who relish control in the way Alecia does.

What I do notice is the lack of affection Jackson displays toward Susan. On several occasions, she places a hand on his arm, and he fails to reciprocate with a touch. In fact, it's as if he doesn't even realize she's there. If my presence doesn't compel the man I want to marry to acknowledge me, he'll be replaced in short order.

The telltale moment happens after they complete the first practice run of their vows, and Alecia, standing in for the minister, says, "You may kiss the bride." Jackson makes no attempt to take advantage of the moment and kiss Susan. She has to flick him on the chest and tell him to kiss her. That's grounds for calling off the wedding. Right?

If I'm putting off marriage while I develop a successful law career, I guaran-darn-tee you the lucky guy I finally pick better kiss me like the end of the world is near every opportunity he gets. Otherwise, why bother with men at all?

Chapter 5

Birmingham is a valley surrounded by small mountains. All the money is earned in the valley. The mountains are where the rich look down and keep an eye on their investments.

Perched precariously on one of the taller mountains is a concrete monstrosity called the Mountain View club. It's a favorite gathering place for the privileged few to enjoy an expensive dinner while lording over the rest of the city.

The Espositos booked a banquet room at the Mountain View club for the after-rehearsal dinner. The check Mr. Esposito must have written to cover the venue and catering would've made a nice dent in my student loans.

Lucky me, I'm trapped between Melissa Owens and a goofy, tall dude from Jackson's party by the name of Joel. Joel has a wedding band on his left hand, not unlike Melissa's diamond on her ring finger. Still, the inconvenient fact they're both married does not prevent them from flirting over my plate. That's unfortunate and slightly nauseating. However, my seat does afford me an excellent view of Jackson during the entire dinner.

Courtney used the term shady to describe Jackson. I can understand how she feels that way from his detached demeanor. He seems to purposefully isolate himself from the festivities. But I'm not ready to condemn him just yet.

It dawns on me; I haven't met Jackson's parents or any siblings. Doesn't he have any, or did they have a lousy relationship, and Jackson decided against inviting them?

Susan's family is tight. The difference between Jackson and

Susan's belief of healthy family interaction could make their marriage difficult. If Jackson becomes needlessly jealous of the Esposito family time—that won't end well.

I want to marry a man with an enormous, super tight family. Face it, marriage is the ultimate trial of getting along with someone for an extended period. Where better for my future husband to hone that skill set than growing up with a bunch of brothers and sisters?

Sister. He can have one sister. She must be sweet.

Mr. Esposito rises and toasts the bride and groom. Mr. E is an incredibly gracious and welcoming man. I can tell he's struggling to say anything nice about his future son-in-law. It's crushing my heart to think he can't be thrilled for his daughter.

During our chicken Cordon Bleu, asparagus, and new potatoes and before the key lime pie, I notice the not-so-well-concealed eye play between Jackson and Mandy Perkins. During the bachelorette party, Mandy kept to herself. She's one of only three women from the groom's party—she claims to be a second cousin to Jackson as I recall.

Those are not second cousin looks the two are sharing. What's up with that?

I scan the rest of the guests to see if anybody else notices the heated eye play between the cousins. Courtney has. Her ears and cheeks are the same red tint as Mandy's short hair.

Courtney notices me looking at her and arches her eyebrows pointedly as if to say, "See what I mean?" Yeah, I do. Even if I don't want to see it. Worse, I'm not sure what it means, given they're supposedly related.

I should've paid more attention to Mandy during the bachelorette party. It would be incredibly helpful right now to know more about her.

My best friend from high school, Jacob Hurley and I use to goof around with sexual innuendos. I decide to cut Jackson and Mandy some slack. Close people sometimes have idiosyncratic ways of interacting that aren't always considered socially normal.

When dessert comes, I change my mind. Mandy either has a

severe case of the shakes or intentionally tries to be sexually provocative. That is, if dabbing meringue on your upper lip and retrieving it with an exaggerated extension of your tongue is sexy.

Mandy appears to think it's sexy. Jackson doesn't seem to mind either. But it makes me ill, and I wish they'd put a lid on it.

When dinner concludes, I see my opening. I slide in next to Mandy as we exit the dining hall. "I hate I didn't get the opportunity to speak with you at the bachelorette party, Mandy."

She glares at me as if I've lost my mind. "Yeah?"

"How are you and Jackson related?"

Her eyes narrow, and I feel her suspicion in the air. "We're family."

Wow. It doesn't get much vaguer than that. "Are Jackson's parents here? I haven't met them yet."

She turns from me as she replies bluntly, "No."

Mandy's hair might be bonfire red, but she plays the ice princess exceptionally well. It's time for more drastic measures. I put my hand on her shoulder as she exits the door. "Do you want to go for drinks with the rest of us?"

The brief porno that flashes through my mind of Mandy and Jackson before she shrugs my unwanted hand off her shoulder suggests the cousins do more than kiss. Worse, my stomach bubbles and churns in repulsion. Not over the voyeuristic porno, I'm not that much of a prude, but the sheer wickedness I feel emanating from her core thoughts and belief system. The only way to describe what I feel when I touch Mandy is evil.

I wouldn't trust Mandy Perkins with my worst enemy. She's the definition of a sociopath and one hundred percent grade 'A' scary.

If Jackson and Mandy are naked-close, all I can think about is my brother Dusty's favorite saying. We are the company we keep. If Jackson is half as bad as Mandy, Susan isn't getting a wedding. She's being sentenced to purgatory.

Mandy rolls her lip into a snarl. "I had enough of your friends last night."

"Did someone say something ugly to you?"

Mandy narrows her eyes, then turns away from me, and double-times her clicking heels toward the exit. I guess our conversation is over.

At eleven-thirty, I send the rest of the girls out of Susan's and my room. The other eleven sorority sisters are chatterboxes tonight. Susan's color has paled, and her eyes are glazing over.

"Thank you," Susan says as I shut the door behind the last of them.

"You're going to be an absolutely beautiful bride tomorrow, but there's no reason to take a chance by not getting any sleep."

"I'm starting to think the whole beauty thing is overrated."

I can't help but laugh at her sad tone, especially when I think about the men in my family. "My brothers and my daddy all say women shouldn't worry about what clothes we have on and how our makeup looks. They claim it has little to no bearing on how they feel about a woman."

"That's not true. I wish it were, but it's not."

"Yeah, you're probably right. The men in my family can be full of it sometimes."

We sit in companionable silence for a few minutes before Susan speaks, "Do you think there's any way to know for sure if Jackson loves me?"

"That's probably a better question to ask your momma or your sister. I haven't even had a guy ever ask me to go exclusive."

"But you know when a guy really likes you, right?"

"Sure. That's an easy one."

Susan scoots to the edge of her bed and leans toward me. "How? How do you know for sure?"

I grin as I look at her sideways. "Their hands usually end up somewhere I don't want them. Or I at least act like I don't want them there."

"That's not what I'm talking about." She throws a pillow at me and misses.

"Okay, I'll play. Tell me how you know Jackson is in love with you."

She looks up to the ceiling as if she's preparing a list. "He certainly doesn't grab me in inappropriate places. He's much too much of a gentleman for that."

That sort of takes the fun out of it and isn't necessarily a good thing. Besides, I'm sure Jackson isn't a gentleman with his supposed, wink wink, second cousin Mandy if grabbing makes you ungentlemanly.

"His attention to detail, for one thing. I've never known a man his age to be so well prepared. He thinks of all the trivial things I haven't considered. It's comforting to know I'm marrying someone who can take care of all the financial issues my dad used to. I don't know anything about money issues, and it doesn't interest me."

I sit up on the edge of my bed. "What do you mean, financial stuff?"

Susan's lips thin, "If I tell you, you have to be quiet about it."

That depends solely on what she tells me, "Sure. You know I can keep a secret."

Susan takes a deep breath, "My dad would absolutely have a fit if he knew we did this before we got married."

If Susan is about to tell me she had premarital sex with Jackson, I don't think her dad will be as shocked as she might believe. It's the twenty-first century, after all. Of course, if she tells me, she's pregnant... But she looks hungry, not pregnant.

"We bought a house together this week."

I struggle to remain neutral. I'm sure my face looks like someone is sticking pins in my skin. "Really? Where? Tell me about it."

Her smile blooms across her face. "It's so beautiful. Never in my wildest dreams did I think I'd own a house like this at my age. But Jackson swears we can afford it. Do you know where Blackstone country club is, outside of Hoover?"

It sounds familiar. "Maybe."

"Jackson and I were able to buy a five-bedroom, four-bath home right off the eleventh hole."

Either my intense dislike for people repeatedly hitting small white balls near my backyard or the thought of an extravagant mortgage is pushing me into total freak out mode. "Why would you hang a huge mortgage around your neck this early in your marriage?"

Susan shrugs. "Jackson says we can afford it. He said it was a steal and a fantastic investment."

I'm beginning to see Susan in a different light. She's incredibly intelligent, but now I realize she is also gullible and slightly lazy. Or, to be fair, just blinded by her love for Jackson.

I wrestle between sharing some of the conspiracy theories my cynical brain has cooked up or minding my own business. But who am I kidding? I never mind my own business.

"Susan, do you think you're stressed because it seems odd Jackson would want you to take on such a huge mortgage before you marry?"

"It was a good deal, April. You have to take a chance and jump on the good deals when they come around." Her eyes narrow, "You think he's shady like everyone else. He's not I tell you. More importantly, he makes me happy!"

Well, that went well. I should've stuck with keeping my mouth shut. "I'm glad you're happy." I fluff my pillow to signal I'm ready to go to sleep. "Do you need anything before I turn the light out?"

She's still shaking from her outburst. I hope it isn't only because she's angry with me. Possibly I was able to sprinkle some reasonable doubt in her mind.

"No." She collapses onto her pillow and turns her back to me.

"Okay. Sleep tight." I flip the light off.

I lay in the dark, staring at the red light from the small microwave oven on the minibar. In vain, I attempt to rationalize every negative impression I formed about Jackson. Everything about Jackson makes me fear for my friend's happiness. Thinking about the man and the implications of Susan marrying him gives me a nauseous feeling in my gut.

I believe I'm an optimistic person, a person who likes to give others the benefit of the doubt. Yet, I'm running out of plausible explanations. Buying a house together before you're married? Who does that? The only thing that could raise more of a red flag is if she told me he bought a life insurance policy on her.

And no family? No grandma or aunt to come to their wedding? Only someone claiming to be his second cousin. A woman with her own secrets, who, if she hasn't slept with Jackson physically, does it routinely in her lurid imagination.

Jackson's phone call just seems to add to the anxious feelings in my stomach. Not that I could really hear what it was about, earlier. Who had he been talking to on his phone? Jackson told them he'd take care of everything. What? Why had his tone been so tense, his inflection strained and hard? It didn't sound like a call to a friend, A business partner, maybe?

Courtney has the right of it. No matter how hard I try to give him the benefit of the doubt, Jackson is just shady. Shady isn't something I want for Susan.

One thing is for sure. Susan isn't going to change her mind about her marriage over any conspiracy theory I cook up. There's only one course of action. I'd have to confront Jackson directly and ask him what sort of game he's playing.

I'll need to be careful. My questioning could set Jackson off. Men like him often go directly to an offended outburst when their motives are questioned. That doesn't bother me. I know it would only be a cover for him having been rightfully accused of unscrupulous behavior.

What does concern me is Susan's reaction when she learns I've been meddling in her affairs without her permission. At the same time, it surprises me I care how she will react since I'm in the right and have her best interest at heart. Wouldn't I be doing her a huge favor? I might be saving her life.

I punch at my pillow again to fluff it. Then I kick my feet out from under the covers. It's going to be a long night.

Chapter 6

The salt from the sea spray collects on my forehead and cheeks. The sun bakes it dry instantaneously into a gritty film. The breeze across my face invigorates me, and the smell of the ocean spray makes me smile.

Leaning against the railing, I watch a fast, sleek pod of porpoises leaping alongside our cruise ship. My thoughts are calm and brimming with hope and happiness.

Sharp pain at the back of my neck explodes throughout my head. I collapse against the railing, and my vision fades until I feel my body rolling over the top bar.

I clutch the railing in alarm, desperate to stop from flipping over. Someone pushes the small of my back while lifting one of my legs. Then I tumble.

The foamy white caps on top of the roiling water speed toward my face. Instinctively my hands stretch in front of me. The diamond on my left-hand catches a beam of light and sparkles like a star seconds before I strike the water.

The water's surface is unforgiving like concrete when my body slaps brutally against it. I plunge into the cold while the water pulls at my garments. All the air rushes from my lungs, I slide deep into the dark depths.

I jerk to a sitting position and pull in a harsh gasp of air. I slap the sheets away from my arms and chest.

My clothes are dry? The panic drains from my mind, and the red numbers from the microwave signal I'm still in my hotel bed.

Patting my hand across the nightstand, I locate my phone and tiptoe to Susan's bed. Scanning the length of Susan with my phone's flashlight, I find all, but her face is tucked into the covers. A twinkle catches my eye, and I flash the light toward Susan's nightstand.

I freeze in terror as I stare at the same shimmering diamond from my dream. My stomach echoes in the silent night as it rumbles irritably.

Things have just gotten real.

Chapter 7

Even Alecia's drill sergeant tactics are of no consequence to me in the morning. I have more pressing issues to deal with than the facade of a perfect wedding.

While the rest of the women in our party enjoy the ladies' only pre-wedding brunch, I'm alone in my mind mulling over my predicament.

My Nana Hirsch, a self-proclaimed witch—and half the town will back her up on the claim—taught me clairvoyant blocking methods when I was eight. It's to help me cope with the freakish mental abilities I inherited genetically from both grandmothers. They call them 'Gifts,' and I call them a personal nightmare.

Usually, the blocking methods work. At the very least, they stop the constant din of voices, from objects strangers have touched, and dead people alike, who would otherwise fill my head.

When blocking methods fail, it usually results in me finding out something embarrassing about another person's thoughts. When this happens, I carry on as if I have zero psychic powers. It isn't difficult to act like I don't know what someone else is thinking since that's the standard expectation of people. This incident with Jackson and his cousin is the first time I've experienced a conflict between ignoring what I've gleaned from another person and doing something with the information.

I want to bury it. I mean, it isn't my responsibility. People make bad decisions all the time. Some even turn them around. Who am I to interfere?

Who am I kidding? I must disprove my suspicions about Jackson and move forward with the wedding in good consciousness or confirm the worst and convince Susan to cancel the event. There'd be no third choice of keeping my mouth shut and hoping for the best.

Being a good friend really bites at times.

I look down the table at Susan, who's chatting merrily with her sister Courtney. Mandy is the only female member of the wedding party unable to attend our late morning get together. Shocking surprise.

Perhaps she's keeping the groom company. I can hope for a little luck, right?

I tap Susan on the shoulder. "I'm going to step outside for a bit of air."

"Are you okay? I know you didn't sleep well last night."

I would've slept better if I hadn't been falling off a cruise ship. "It's just a bit stuffy in here."

As I start out of the dining hall, I take one last look at the cupcakes at the end of the breakfast bar. My willpower flags and I pick up one of the softball-sized delicacies.

I devour the scrumptious treat as I backtrack down the hotel hall to the wing the men were assigned. I slow down as I pass Jackson's room. Nothing. No TV, no voices, and of all the rotten luck, no grunting or screams of pleasure.

After reassuring myself nobody is around, I put my ear to his door. Still no screams of exaltation.

So much for an easy out. I'll have to work for this one.

I continue down the hallway past the registrar's counter and out the glass double doors—and run right into my prey. Mandy lurks on the other side of the column sitting on a small bench, and I would've missed her if I didn't smell the cigarette smoke. She takes a long drag on her menthol as she bounces her foot anxiously in the air.

"You aren't hungry?"

Mandy jerks her head toward me. She recognizes me and blows a long smoky snake out of her mouth. "I'm not much of a breakfast person."

Not much of a people person, either. "Oh, I wish I had your will-power. Bacon and waffles are hard to lay off."

Mandy rolls her eyes as she takes another drag.

"Have you ever tried to quit?"

She blows smoke out her nostrils before she answers. "Why would I?"

I'm about to explain to Mandy the harsh realities of lung cancer but decide she should smoke an extra pack a day.

"Have you seen Jackson today?"

She sighs loudly. "Why?"

"I need to talk to him about something. Something about the wedding."

"It wasn't my day to keep up with him." She crushes the spent cigarette with her heel.

I'm not slow to take a hint, but it aggravates me when people don't want to talk to me. Sometimes I get my joy by provoking them right back. I'm sure Mandy is thinking of my face as she crushes the cigarette stub. The feeling is mutual. But since the day is supposed to be a joyous occasion, I let it slide.

She stands to leave. Peppering her with more questions isn't going to get me anywhere. To reach any resolution, I need to confront Jackson.

I wander back into the dining area where the hotel held our all girl's brunch. Most everyone has cleared out except the two Esposito sisters.

"Better?" Susan asks me with a smile.

"Much." Now that I'd left Mandy behind.

Maisie begins to cry in Courtney's arms. "Whoops. It looks like someone is ready for her brunch." Courtney says.

"Well, she is one of the girls," Susan remarks.

Courtney stands and repositions Maisie in her arms. She leans over and kisses Susan on the head. "I'm going back to the room to feed her. I'm more comfortable there."

"Okay. I'll see you back in the dressing room at two."

We both watch Courtney retreat down the hallway, rocking

Maisie as she goes.

"Do you think Maisie will let her get through the ceremony?"

I shrug, "She's a baby. They're unpredictable. I give it a fifty-fifty chance."

Susan favors me a grin. "You're being generous. But it wouldn't bother me even if she acts up during the ceremony. It'll be neat to tell her she was here when I was married, even if she can't remember it because she's too little."

I hoped to discuss with Susan the weird interactions I observed between Jackson and Mandy last night. The chicken in me still believes Susan might suddenly snap to her senses and understand her family's and my concerns about her fiancé.

Deep down, I know I'm delusional if I believe she will come to her senses on her own. Direct intervention will be the only way to save her from herself.

It's as if Susan is defined by the wedding ceremony itself and hasn't paid attention to the most crucial part of the event. The schmuck she plans to marry.

"Have you seen Jackson this morning?" I ask.

She rolls her lower lip out at me. "Lord, I hope not. It would be bad luck."

Man, I'm an idiot.

"All the boys went to play golf early this morning. He should be back within the hour." Her expression changes. "Why do you ask?"

That's a good and unexpected question, "I was just wondering, with Jackson being a financial advisor, if he had any tips on life insurance." Where did that come from?

"Why do you need life insurance?"

I can feel my skin turning red, and I'm fighting not to smile. I am officially the world's worst liar. "I heard if you buy it before you need it, you can get it cheaper."

"Yeah. I remember Jackson saying it's a lot cheaper when you're younger."

My curiosity snaps to attention. I try to remain nonchalant. "Is that what Jackson tells his clients to get them to purchase insurance?"

Susan giggles, "I don't know what he tells his clients. I just know that's what he said when we got ours."

So many alarms go off in my head. I sway with dizziness. *Please no, Susan. Please tell me you didn't.* "You both bought life insurance?"

"Well, duh, silly. It's an important building block of your financial future. I mean, we just bought a house together. If something happened to one of us, we would want the other one to not have to sell the house."

My breathing begins to mimic a dog panting.

"Jackson is so sweet. He made mine a million dollars. He said it was way too low because I'm priceless, and he doubts he would be able to live without me. He made me put my parent's as secondary benefactors in case he dies of a broken heart before my policy pays out." I swear the blissful look she gives me has me thinking she's downed a fistful of pain killers while I was outdoors. "Isn't he the sweetest?"

Jackson's so full of crap his eyes are brown. "He's definitely a charmer."

"He's charmed my heart. I can't wait to start our new life together."

That's a lovely sentiment, but I'm becoming concerned about how long that new life might last.

My window of opportunity is closing quickly. I have one shot to pull Jackson away from the masculine crew before the wedding. If I don't catch him coming back from the golf outing, he'll be comfortably surrounded by men in the groom's room. I won't have the opportunity to speak to him privately.

I have no choice but to stake out at the front of the hotel and wait for the men's return from the golf outing.

One of the hotel shuttles pulls up, and men from our wedding, many I met for the first time the night before, begin to pour out of the minibus. Mr. Esposito steps off the bus laughing with one of the other men, easily thirty years his junior. They collect their golf bags as the driver sets them off the bus.

I'm shocked. Jackson invited Mr. Esposito to go with the younger crowd. How cold-blooded do you have to be to bond with a parent when you plan their child harm? The depths of Jackson's evil is unfathomable. Still, I hold some hope that my cynical overactive imagination might be mistaken.

"April? Shouldn't you be with Susan?" Mr. Esposito asks.

"Alecia ran me out," I answer, "we're getting close to the witching hour, and she'll be a control freak for the rest of the ceremony."

Mr. Esposito nods his head. "I suppose that's what I pay her for."

"And I'd say you're going to get your money's worth."

Jackson and his best man Noel Winger are the last two to exit the bus. Jackson hands the driver several bills as a tip.

Unable to disguise the displeasure that flashes across his face when he realizes I'm waiting on him, Jackson taps Noel on the shoulder and gestures with his head in my direction. Noel looks like he's sizing me up for a body bag as he passes by me.

"I don't feel the need to explain myself to you, but in the interest of keeping the peace, we probably should talk," Jackson says.

Wow. Direct and to the point. I usually appreciate that quality in people. Unfortunately, Jackson has the drop on me and has initiated the conversation before I could. "In the interest of keeping the peace, yes, let's talk."

Jackson eyes an older couple walking out of the double glass doors. "Let's talk over here."

I follow his lead to a grouping of live oaks at the front of the parking lot. Briefly, I consider cutting to the chase by touching him. It would be useful to read his current thoughts. I decide to go with my original plan and hit the record button on my phone as I cross my arms.

"Susan called me and told me she mentioned the house we purchased together and that you took exception to it." His jaw muscle clenches as a vein pops up at his temple.

"I just can't understand why a new couple would want to burden themselves with a mortgage that size."

Jackson's eyes bore into me. "I'm trying to think who you are to worry about it?"

His delivery is as good as a sharp slap to my face, and I stammer, "a good friend of Susan's."

"Good friends don't take a dump in the punch bowl at your wedding."

Classy. "Friends would if it meant saving your life."

Jackson chuckles. His display of fake amusement chills my blood. "Now you're saving lives? That's a bit dramatic, isn't it? I've never known anyone to die over a mortgage payment."

My ire bubbles over. Common sense tells me Jackson is too big for me to knock on his fanny while my heart tells me I'd prefer to go down swinging than suffer his condescending smirks any longer.

"It's not dramatic if it's true." I step closer to him, and he leans back slightly. "Is it true? Should I be worried about Susan's health?"

"Are you for real? Do you even hear yourself? Do you hear how illogical you sound?"

"I'm just asking an honest question. An honest question you seem ready to deflect rather than answer."

"Because it's preposterous. Why are you asking me something that disgusting?"

I shake my head slowly. "Because I think you're hiding something."

"You've got nothing. You're crazy."

"I'm crazy?" I raise my eyebrows, "I'm not the one purchasing a house in Blackstone on the down-low before I'm married. That's one heck of a starter home, Jackson."

His face flushes red. He appears to be finally losing his cool with me. "That house was an excellent buy."

"Maybe for someone who has an income."

His eyes widen, and his nostrils flare. "Who are you, the house dictator? Like I said, it was a good deal. As for my income, you have no idea."

"If it is such a good deal, why don't you share the great news with Mr. Esposito? I'm sure he would love to hear about this awesome deal his future son-in-law pulled off."

"It wasn't like that. Esposito wouldn't understand. Bargains like that must be closed on immediately. They don't always fit nicely with everybody's preconceived notion and timetables."

I watch the slight bit of spittle on his lower lip roll to his chin. I'm done giving passes. It's time to burn bridges.

"Somehow, I think you may be able to get the Espositos to understand the purchase of your new house, but you won't be able to convince them of the need for a million-dollar life insurance policy on their daughter."

Jackson's face turns a ghastly shade of purplish-red at once. We glare at each other without speaking for a minute. Jackson breaks the stare-off first.

"I don't know who you think you are coming here, passing judgment on Susan and my decisions. That's what couples do. They make decisions together to better their lives. I can see how you might be jealous of us since you don't have a man, which is no big surprise considering you're a royal pain in the butt, but you need to get over yourself."

Jackson's words temporarily addle my senses. This character is a piece of work. I take a deep breath and gather myself as I remember this isn't about me. This is about Susan and her future.

"Personally, I'm not interested in whether you do or don't like me. But I am interested in Susan's wellbeing, and I believe her parents will be highly interested to hear what you've been up to. If you'll excuse me, I need to have a discussion with them."

I turn on my heel but am jerked back by my wrist. Jackson crushes my arm against his chest, our faces are inches apart and my phone is against his neck. He speaks through clenched teeth as vivid visions crash through my mind, threatening to unhinge my knees and irreparably bend my consciousness.

The vision of a kitchen table covered in translucent plastic smeared with thick crimson jelly is so realistic I smell the scent of blood in the air. The hacksaw balanced precariously on the table's edge, gore and hair attached to the blade, drips blood slowly to the beige tile below.

"You need to watch yourself. If I were you, I wouldn't worry about Susan. I'd worry about you."

My lungs constrict with fear and a trickle of sweat tracks down my spine. Despite my terror, my smart mouth takes over. "Is that a threat, Jackson? I sure hope so."

His eyes narrow, and he pinches my wrist tighter, his nails biting into my skin before he pushes my arm away from him. "Let's just call it some excellent advice from your friend's husband."

Funny, the last I checked, nobody was married yet. Like they say, it's not over until the fat lady sings. I'm not especially fat, but the engagement is going to be over once I get to singing. Jackson isn't going to like my tune one bit.

Chapter 8

It's been five hours since I confronted Jackson, and I still don't know what to do with the case I've built against him. Remaining silent as we near the wedding tortures me. I've all the confirmation I need that Jackson is working a scam that includes the murder of Susan for financial gain.

But it's a case I've built on circumstantial evidence.

I've replayed the tape I made of Jackson. While what he says makes me madder than a wet hen, he never says anything incriminating. I'm aware if this were a court of law, I'd not move forward with prosecution because no jury would convict Jackson with the evidence I currently possess. The jury would have to liberally color in the rest of the case with cynical conjecture and a healthy appreciation for conspiracy theories to return a guilty verdict.

But this isn't a court of law. This is more like a civil trial. I may only need to prove that there is a high likelihood that something is amiss with the union. Safety must be paramount to proving beyond a shadow of a doubt. Right?

The problem is Judge Susan will be issuing the ruling on this case. There's no way I can convince Susan her charming Jackson has laid this sinister trap for her. Heck, if I didn't have firsthand knowledge of the evil inside Jackson, I'd have a difficult time believing it too.

I need a new venue for this case. I need Judge Susan to recuse herself.

Briefly, I consider dumping it on Courtney. It's a family thing. Right?

Bless it. What's wrong with me? When did I become such a chicken?

In my heart, I know the family has seen issues with Jackson all along, and they've been unable to convince her. If they had the power to change her mind, they would have done it long before going through the trouble and expense of this spectacle of a ceremony.

No. If anyone derails this nightmare train, it needs to be me. For one, I'm not blood. I won't have to deal with awkward family get-togethers if I ruin the wedding. The Esposito sisters would.

Still, the nagging desire to bury my head in the sand and pretend I don't know the details of Jackson's evil plans continues. *Just be normal, April. Nobody would ever expect you had prior knowledge.*

I'd know. How will it affect me if the worst does happen to Susan?

It comes down to one fundamental question. The problem being I don't know how I will answer it. My decision changes minute to minute during my raging internal debate. The competing counselors in my head, 'Mr. Shut Your Mouth' and 'Ms. Save A Friend', are both litigating their cases with excellent skill and merit.

The single tough question remains: As the prosecutor, I'll have to decide whether to bring the case to the jury or let it lie. Then I must live with my decision.

Is Susan a good enough friend for me to blow up her wedding and become a social outcast to save her from marrying Jackson?

I'm just not sure.

We put on our powder blue bridesmaid dresses and help Susan into her stunning wedding gown. It's all I can do to hold the smile on my face and not erupt into tears. She's genuinely in love. Susan is practically glowing with excitement. I hold the devastating news that will crush her dream like a discarded cigarette.

The organ plays the first notes of the ceremony. The crass sound signals my time for deliberation is over, and I must make an impossible decision where both options have horrific implications.

Mrs. Esposito opens a couple bottles of Pinot Noir to calm everyone's nerves. I, as a result, down more than my share pondering the undesirable responsibility my oddity has created.

Why can't I just be normal? If I were normal, I wouldn't have to deal with this hopeless decision.

The vision from last night's nightmare flashes in my mind. The one where I'm falling toward the ocean with my hands out to break my fall. It occurs to me the hands with the large diamond ring in the vision are smaller and fairer than mine. The diamond that sparkled just before being swallowed by the dark depths of the cold ocean is presently on Susan's left hand.

The vision is followed in short order by the plastic covered kitchen table. It's a murderer's attempt to dispose of a body, but whose? Susan's body would be lost to the ocean and ruled an accident, I'm sure.

For all my complaining, it's better to know. Knowledge is power. Yet power can weigh heavily on one's mind.

Alecia enters the bride's chamber. She claps her hands twice. "All right, ladies. It's time to get in line with the ushers."

Alecia regards Susan, standing in front of the mirror with her delicate hands pensively laced in front of her. "You're absolutely stunning, Susan."

The compliment brings even deeper color to Susan's wine, blushed cheeks. "Thank you, Alecia."

I just can't. How can I ruin my friend's perfect day?

Since my discussion with Jackson, I've been searching for an alternative method to protect Susan. I wish there were a way to extract her from the doomed marriage without scarring her socially forever. I'd be all for it. The problem is I can't think of a single thing.

No. I can't do it. Call me weak, spineless, or just a gutless friend. But in my mind, this train has left the station. It's pointless for me to hop up on the track and try to stop the train. If I do that, I'll be splatted on the grill of the locomotive like a cicada.

Sabotaging a friend's wedding day is a serious faux pas. Susan, as sweet as she is, will probably just ban me from her life. Me? If someone ruined my day, I'd exact a pound of flesh. The friend who blows up my wedding shouldn't be surprised when the expensive shampoo sample that came in the mail makes her hair fall out in clumps. At the same time, her ex-lovers begin calling and asking about the sexually transmitted disease the health department says she gave them.

Alecia marches everyone out of the room except for Mrs. Esposito and Susan. We line up with the ushers we paired with at rehearsal.

My usher, Lonnie, scans my dress and curls his upper lip. "Geez, I feel bad about throwing a fit over having to wear a powder blue cummerbund."

"Really, dude? Just don't." I give him an extra-strong dose of the 'Crazy Eyes.' I'm in no mood for chit chat.

Lonnie does a double-take and crosses his hands in front of his crotch. I think it's a nervous habit of his. He can't have thought I'd hit him there. I don't know him like that.

The organ starts into the music that keys our entrance to the chapel. Alecia claps her hands. "All right, here we go. Here we go. Edward and Bonnie lead us out."

Lonnie and I are the last bridesmaid and usher. When I take his arm, I sense fear, anxiety, and confusion. I pull back on my energy levels. The last thing I need is to find out Lonnie is also planning to murder someone, and I need to rat him out too.

As Courtney releases Noel's arm to take their places on opposite sides of the altar, Jackson comes into view. Why did I ever cut him any slack? I don't need the ability to read his thoughts. The knowing smirk fixed on his face tells me all I need to know about him. He looks like someone who knows he's getting away with a crime.

Oh, snap. If I don't blow up this wedding, Jackson will be getting away with his devious plan.

I don't have a choice. There is no way I can let Susan go through with this sham. I can't allow her to be in harm's way. My minor social pain is nothing compared to her life.

When Lonnie and I reach the front of the chapel, we separate.

Rather than fall in line with the bridesmaids, I take a wide path around them, looping back toward the altar.

The first notes of the wedding march thunder through the sanctuary.

I trot the last few steps to the organ and pull the microphone from its stand.

"Wait a second, y'all. I have something important to tell you."

Susan and her daddy are at the chapel entrance. She's so incredibly beautiful, her long flowing dress perfection. Her daddy's eyebrows push together in confusion.

"I know we're supposed to be quiet until the preacher asks if anybody has any objections. But I'm afraid this one can't wait." Jackson starts to move toward me in my peripheral. I calculate I've only seconds to finish my business.

"First off, I want to thank the Esposito family for a wonderful party and this beautiful ceremony. Unfortunately, Susan's fiancé, Jackson, is planning to kill her on their honeymoon."

The faces of the wedding guests from my vantage register an odd mixture of horror and complete confusion. "True story. But you don't have to believe me, you can listen for yourself." I pull my phone from between my breasts and hit the play button.

"It wasn't like that. Esposito wouldn't understand. Bargains like that must be closed on immediately. They don't always fit nicely with everybody's preconceived notion and timetables."

Jackson's voice is more discernable than I dared to hope. I turn the recording up to its loudest volume and hold it inches from the microphone.

"Somehow, I think you may be able to get the Espositos to understand the purchase of your new house, but you won't be able to convince them of the need for a million-dollar life insurance policy on their daughter."

Jackson pulls up short of me and raises his hands toward the audience as a loud cacophony of gasps and grumbles comes from the crowd. "It's just a joke, folks. That's all. A wedding prank."

While the recording continues to play, Jackson stammers, attempting to explain away the joke as a simple dare from his friends. From the guests' expressions, including the groom's party, they aren't buying his explanation.

"You need to watch yourself. If I were you, I wouldn't worry about Susan. I'd worry about you."

The guests' expressions switch from confusion to concern and anger. A few stand as if they're contemplating moving toward the altar.

"Is that a threat, Jackson? I sure hope so."

Mr. Esposito has left Susan's side and is jogging toward the altar.

"Let's just call it some excellent advice from your friend's husband."

It isn't a confession in the purest sense. But it seems close enough for the guests as they glower at Jackson. The energy in the room gives off a dangerous crackling noise.

As the last of the recording plays, I scan the sanctuary. Mr. Esposito vaults up the altar steps toward Jackson as Susan falls to her knees with a sob that sounds like a wild animal trapped in a snare.

My worst fears are confirmed. There will be no coming back from this social faux pas, ever. I've no hope nor expectation of being a bridesmaid for the twenty-fourth time.

Somehow, I'm okay with that.

I raise the microphone to eye level. Then I drop it.

April May Snow is done with weddings.

Mr. Esposito grabs Jackson by the lapels of his tuxedo as several other guests stream toward the two men. Their voices already developing into an unintelligible roar.

Mrs. Esposito and Courtney make their way to the back of the chapel, where Susan lays crumpled on the floor. She's sobbing uncontrollably, but she's alive, and the people who love her will see her through this tragedy. At least that's what I tell myself to not feel like I'm the worst friend ever.

Oh well. If the goal today were to blow up my friend's wedding ceremony, I'd say I've done an exceptional job. It's time for me to take my leave before anyone notices I'm still here.

Leaving by the choir exit off the stage, I race back to the bride's chamber to collect my purse and street clothes. I can hear the sanctuary erupting into an even louder pitched thunder of commotion.

I half figure I'll hear the organ belt out the bridal march again. After allowing a few minutes for things to calm down, Jackson may be able to convince them what they heard was just the ramblings of a disturbed woman?

It's Susan's decision now. She has all the information, and what happens now is not on me. My conscience is clear.

Quickly I step out of my dress and yank my cotton sundress over my head. I gather the rest of my belongings. I hesitate as I pull the protective covering over my bridesmaid dress.

Screw it. I'll never have an occasion to wear it again. I toss it on the small sofa, but I grab my shoes by their heels. They are so cute. I can wear them again.

Slipping out the large double doors, I double-time it to my car. I need to make myself scarce as soon as possible.

I speed my car out of the church parking lot a little too fast as I debate my destination. I don't have a class until Tuesday. Returning to Tuscaloosa and sitting in my apartment alone for three days doesn't seem like a plan. It would be too much time for self-loathing, and I feel my emotions getting away from me as the adrenaline high dissipates.

The Gulf Coast is only five hours away. I could be there before midnight. Some sand in between my toes would go a long way toward easing my troubled mind.

But there, too, I'd be alone. I'd have ample time to reflect on the fact I'm a freak of nature and a lousy person who ruined my friend's wedding.

The beach is out.

As I drive, I can't help but replay the events over and over in my head. Did I have another play? Should I have talked to Susan's parents first?

There was no other way. I'd done the only thing I could given the situation.

Besides, I'm not the issue, Jackson's the problem. Still, we'll both be cast into the wilderness. Granny Snow always likes to joke, "No good deed goes unpunished."

Doing the right thing can really suck is my translation.

As if on autopilot, my car takes the ramp onto interstate fifty-nine. The lonely asphalt miles bracketed by tall pine trees pass, and eventually, I find myself in Guntersville. Crazy. I guess I can use a boat ride on the lake and a conversation with my family. Mama and Daddy will appreciate the surprise.

My spirits lift more than I anticipated when I pull up my parent's drive. I can see the kitchen light on through the sliding glass door.

I check my phone before I head into my parent's home. I have a single text message. It's from Courtney.

'I can only hope to raise Maisie to be half as brave as you. Thank you for being courageous enough to save my sister's life today. I am forever in your debt.'

The tears welling in my eyes catch me by surprise. I guess doing the right thing does have its own reward.

The End

If you enjoyed the short story <u>Throw the Bouquet</u>, please leave a review. Reviews are a tremendous way to help the authors you enjoy.
https://www.amazon.com/gp/product/B07PHQQLTR

Please turn the page for a sample from
The novella, <u>Throw the Cap</u>, the 2nd entry in the
April May Snow Psychic Adventure series.

Throw the Cap

Chapter 1

I finished proofing my case study answers for the second time and laid my pencil down. Fifteen minutes of test time remained according to the clock on the wall.

Proof the answers a third time? Yeah, not part of the plan today. I only needed to pass. I'd given up on perfection since receiving a job offer from Master, Johnson, and Lloyd.

I couldn't contain a self-satisfied grin. April May Snow finished law school, and I stood at the start of my spectacular new life.

I completed the last final of the last class of my third year of law school. Unless a future case of temporary insanity hit me, my days of formal education were complete.

Hey, don't misunderstand. The University of Alabama proved to be a blast. But I bet even Heaven is a drag after the seventh year.

College has been more fun than my wildest dreams. I needed to start making some money fast. The banks holding my student loans send me friendly reminders daily, telling me they own a generous portion of any income I earned.

Knowing the banks' names were basically written on my pay stubs, doesn't make me happy.

What made me happy? The idea of my future job in Atlanta. I'd worked my tail off the last seven years to land a position with a prestigious law firm.

I glanced over to my study buddy Martin Culp. When I raised my brow to inquire how he thought he fared, he jigged his hand in the air and feigned a yawn. Martin might be a goober at times, but he's my best friend and a fantastic study partner.

He tipped his hand up in front of his lips. Drinks? Ugh. I supposed the proper etiquette after completing the final exam of a three-year program would be to celebrate. With graduation in three days, my parents due in, operating on only two hours of sleep last night, I needed to go home, clean up the apartment, and take a nap. After the previous seven years partying might've been my major, so the last thing I should need is a drink. Besides noon might be too early to start drinking.

I winked at Martin and gave him a thumbs up.

Hey, don't judge. This might be the last time I got to share a drink with my classmates.

Dr. Rosenstein strode toward the podium. His slight build and hunched shoulders crunched his tall form into one appearing to be small and passive. His rich reddish-brown and gray hair curled in thick unruly shocks.

If not for Rosenstein, I wouldn't be completing law school.

When starting at Alabama, I'd considered following in the footsteps of my daddy, the engineer. By the end of my freshman year, I realized I couldn't hack all the math and science required for an engineering degree. I can do math and science with the best of them. But those two subjects required a tremendous amount of homework.

Homework really interfered with my underage drinking and partying.

Clearly, I needed a new major. I'd considered accounting but took too long to make up my mind and all the courses filled.

In his twenties and thirties, Rosenstein excelled as a high-powered defense attorney in LA. He'd already hit his late forties and become the Assistant Dean of the law school by the time I met him.

It was quite unusual for a professor of his stature to take on any undergraduate classes. Graduate instructors typically didn't like mixing with the unwashed masses.

But Rosenstein insisted on instructing one undergraduate class a year. Said he liked to have some interaction with students before four years of political correctness had them regurgitating the clone-like dialect.

He said it also allowed him to recruit students who should consider a law career. That semester Rosenstein worked overtime convincing me I was a lawyer at heart and specifically a litigator.

In retrospect, I must admit he hit the nail on the head. With each passing year and class, I became increasingly confident about my choice of profession.

It wasn't like I'd never considered the career before Rosenstein recruited me to the profession. After all, my Uncle, Howard Snow, has a successful practice in my hometown of Guntersville, Alabama.

But without Rosenstein's insistence and affirmation, I wouldn't have chosen a law career. Why would I select a career that required me to apply myself as much as I'd had to the six years since I took the decision? I mean, that's why I'd ditched engineering. Right?

I felt blitzed before Martin even appeared to have a buzz. He was drinking beer, and I was drinking red wine. One of these days, I would learn how to sip my Merlot instead of downing it like shots.

"I'm going to call for a ride home and take a nap," I announced.

Martin rolled his head to the right. "C'mon, Snow. Don't wimp out on me. We got all night to celebrate."

"I'm operating on two hours' sleep. I've got to clean up my place before my parents get here, and I promised Breanna I would help the sorority decorate the house tomorrow." I narrowed my eyes. "Besides, don't you have some girlfriend you need to hook up with?"

Martin was dating a cute sophomore by the name of Penny Trickett. I liked to give him a tough time about having to tuck her in at night and make sure she said her prayers before she went to bed.

I didn't care one way or the other that there were five years between their ages since they were both adults. I only brought it up because I liked to kid Martin, and he was fun to aggravate.

"She's in a tutoring session that lasts until ten."

"She must be as dumb as a box of rocks if she needs a tutoring session that long. And here I thought you said she was smart. Besides dating you, of course."

"She's teaching the tutoring session."

Whoops. I blew that one. "As if."

"What do you care anyway?" Martin sulked.

I couldn't help but laugh, "Because you implied that I need to stay here as long as you're drinking. There's no way I'm drinking with you until ten PM."

"Then invite me over to watch TV while you sleep."

My face twisted in repulsion. "No way."

He shrugged. "I'll bring my own beer."

"Drink your beer in your own apartment."

"But there's nobody there. It's depressing to drink alone."

For being so smart, Martin could be incredibly stupid. "You'd be drinking alone at my place, too. I'll be in bed."

His eyes opened wide, "You're really not going to let me come over?"

I couldn't help but giggle. "No, you idiot."

"Man, that's a sorry way to treat a friend."

Chapter 2

My stomach grumbled so loud it woke me up. I checked the clock. Seven PM. No wonder I was hungry.

I padded to my kitchen. When I exited my bedroom, Martin was on my sofa sleeping off his beer.

Darn it. I forgot I had told Martin he could come over.

I examined myself—basketball shorts and a sports bra. I thought about grabbing a T-shirt, but it was just Martin. I could walk nude to the fridge, and Martin wouldn't notice. Besides, my sugar level was crashing hard.

Foraging in my refrigerator, followed by my cupboard, was

not as fruitful as I had hoped. I was moving out of my apartment next week and had purposely let my food supplies dwindle. The logic had been sound until now.

Great, that meant I was going to have to drag myself back out of my apartment. I scanned the kitchen and living room to ascertain the required minimum amount of cleaning before my family arrived. It wasn't so bad. Oh, who was I kidding? It was a pigsty, and that's before I got to the Prince Harry look alike beer-snoring on my sofa.

After pulling on a T-shirt, I rocked Martin's shoulder. "Hey. You want to go get a burger?"

Martin sat up and rubbed the sleep out of his eyes, "I'm sorry. I didn't mean to fall asleep. What time is it?"

"About seven-thirty. You hungry?"

"Okay. Bubba John's?"

I was thinking something a little more basic and a lot more conservative on the calories. Bubba John's specializes in fusion burger monstrosities. But hey, it might be the last time I ever ate a Bubba John's.

Bubba John's should sell golf carts. They would make a mint. A golf cart was the only way I could've gotten back to my apartment after dinner. I was as full as a tick.

Bubba John's caters to the male crowd, where quantity was equally as important as the price. It's impossible to resist a half-pound burger with double cheese topped with a half-pound of barbecue pork, three slices of bacon, and coleslaw, all for the low price of five dollars. It's too good of a deal not to buy even if you can't eat all of it.

I understood the concept that I only had to eat what I wanted. The problem was that—even though I had the right to stop when I was full—I rarely had the discipline to stop.

Martin recounted the entire final exam while we waited for

our food to settle. Sometimes it amazed me how efficiently his mind could retain the smallest of detail. Me, not so much. Not because I don't have a good memory. I do. It was that my interest button was sort of broke. There were a lot of things I didn't care much about anymore.

"One thing's for sure. Old Rosenstein is going soft. His tests aren't half as difficult as they used to be."

"Maybe you're just twice as smart as you used to be."

Martin's face tightened as he considered the point. "You think so?"

I dabbed at the condensation ring my glass had left on the table. "Nah." I broke into a laugh as I watched his eyes narrow.

"I am not going to miss you busting my balls, Snow."

"Oh, you'll miss me."

"Honestly, I don't think so."

I gained control of my laughter. "Are you still going up to DC?"

"All set."

It had always been Martin's dream to move to Washington, D.C., and work in and around politics. I used to kid him that he should have gone to an Ivy League school, Lord knows he was smart enough. I thought nobody up there would hire a kid from the U of A.

Apparently, yes. Last month Representative Weber from the fourth District had offered him an internship.

"I hate to think that one of my friends is crossing over to the dark side."

"I'm not going to the dark side. I'm bringing the light to run all the cockroaches out. You watch. I'm going to bring respectability back to DC politics."

"At this stage, that would be a tall order for God."

"Well, hopefully, he'll help a little."

He'd have to. Martin was smart and capable but had zero street smarts. There wasn't a single scenario in my mind where he wasn't swallowed up by that city of egomaniacs. Martin was too sweet and always looking to work as a team.

"You'll have to call me occasionally. I want to hear you brag about how many cockroaches you ran out of town."

Martin smiled, exposing the dimple in his right cheek. "I'll have my assistant call and check up on you in your corner office in Atlanta."

"That's big of you." I was going to miss Martin. I was going to miss having someone to talk to that I didn't have to worry about how they were going to take what I said. Martin and I were both given to wisecracks, and we were rarely judgmental.

No, it wasn't as odd as you think that my best friend happened to be a guy. I had two brothers and no sisters. I felt more comfortable talking to guys than I do to women, even my sisters, from the sorority.

I had friends that were female. It was just that sometimes worrying about how they might take my jokes was exhausting. Not to mention, a few of them seemed to live for creating drama. I didn't have the energy for drama anymore.

I wondered who my friends would be in Atlanta. My eyelids drooped. "What time is it?"

Martin and I went for our phones at the same time. "Hello, where did the time go? It's ten-thirty." Martin said as his eyes opened comically wide.

"Ooh. Penny's going to be mad at you." I shook my finger at him. "No sex for you."

"That's what she'll be saying on the phone. She'll change her mind once she sees me." He pushed back his chair and dropped twenty dollars on the table.

"Why? Do you have a Channing Tatum outfit in your car?"

"Funny. Believe it or not, some women find me attractive."

I feigned confusion. "Really? Is this with the lights on or off?"

"Sticks and stones, Snow. I'll catch up with you tomorrow."

"See you later, Martin."

As I watched my broad-shouldered friend exit the bar, I wondered if Penny knew how good she had it. She was a lucky girl to have such a great guy already thinking about the long game with her.

I guess it was lucky for Martin, too. He was the marrying type. Another reason why the whole DC thing had never made sense to me. But you could only point out the obvious so many times to a friend before you started to irritate them.

He was a smart guy. If he wanted it bad enough, he'd figure out how to have his dream job and his dream family.

Me? I was going to head over to Atlanta and become the most sought-after corporate litigator in the Southeast. Nah, make it in the country. Why limit your goals?

Chapter 3

I had passed out on my sofa, watching Lord of the Rings for the thirtieth time when my phone rang. My caller ID indicated Martin. "Hey, what's up?"

"Penny never showed."

If it weren't for the near panic tone in his voice, I would have joked about the situation. "And she's not answering her phone?"

"No. She's not answering my texts, either."

Not good.

Click below to continue reading Throw the Cap

https://www.amazon.com/gp/product/B07PHRCLSB

Author's Note

Thank you for taking the time to read another April May Snow story. I understand there are thousands of books available to you and am humbled you selected one of April's stories to read. I hope you're enjoying reading about her life. Thank you!

I'd like to encourage you to post a review in Amazon. A single sentence review from you is a powerful way to support authors you enjoy. It allows our books to be found by additional readers and frankly motivates us to continue to produce stories. This is especially true for your independents.

A little backstory on the April May Snow platform. The stories from the <u>Throw the</u> series are all prequels to the <u>Foolish</u> series which are full length novels. I hope you continue the journey with April and me.

Once again thank you for your support. You make this adventure possible.

M. Scott Swanson

Do you want to stay in touch with April May? Turn the page.

M. Scott Swanson lives in Nashville, TN. with his wife and two guard chihuahuas. When he's not writing, he's cooking, coaching little league soccer or taking long walks to smooth out plot lines for the next April May Snow adventure.

Want to stay in touch? Don't forget to follow and like.

https://www.amazon.com/-/e/B07PKCPR5T

https://www.facebook.com/mscottswanson/

https://www.goodreads.com/author/show/19074534.M_Scott_Swanson

mscottswanson@gmail.com

Don't forget to sign up for the mail list at https://www.mscottswanson.com/

Thank you for your support!

Made in the USA
Monee, IL
07 January 2021